Bluebell Woods

Natalie's Winter Wonderland

For my daughter,
Jo Shepperd, with love.
L.N.

For Nat, and the girls,
Lily and Yasmin XXX
R.H

STRIPES PUBLISHING
An imprint of Magi Publications
1 The Coda Centre, 189 Munster Road,
London SW6 6AW

A paperback original
First published in Great Britain in 2011

Text copyright © Liss Norton, 2011
Illustrations copyright © Rebecca Harry, 2

ISBN: 978-1-84715-195-7

A CIP catalogue record for this book is available
from the British Library.

Printed and bound in China.

STP/1800/0004/0611

10 9 8 7 6 5 4 3 2 1

Bluebell Woods

Natalie's Winter Wonderland

Liss Norton
Illustrated by Rebecca Harry

stripes

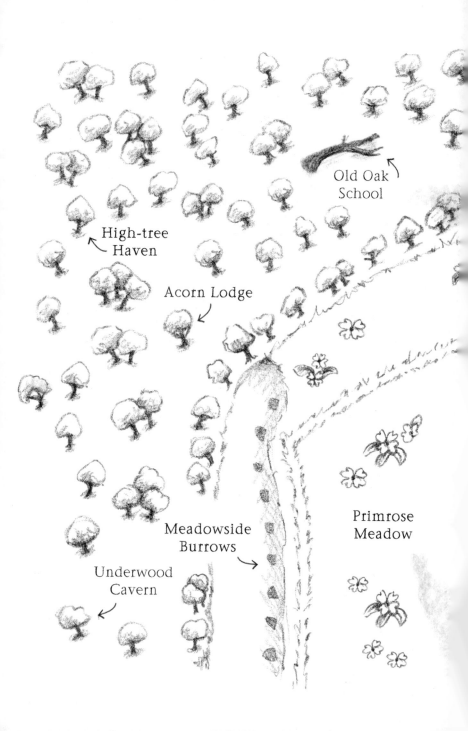

Old Oak
School

High-tree
Haven

Acorn Lodge

Meadowside
Burrows

Underwood
Cavern

Primrose
Meadow

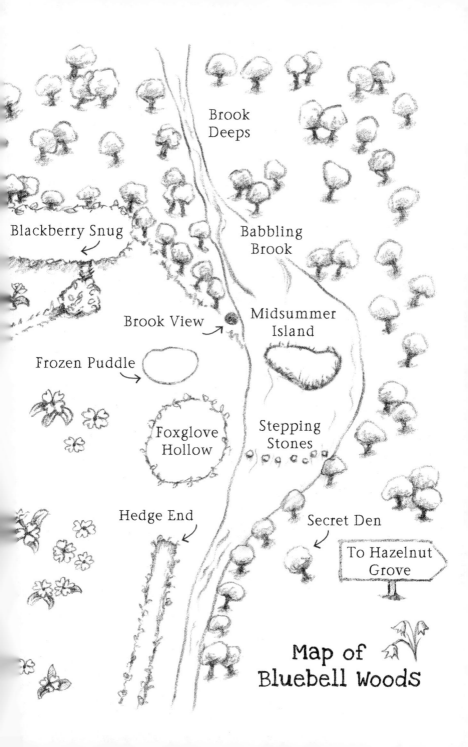

Brook
Deeps

Blackberry Snug

Babbling
Brook

Brook View

Midsummer
Island

Frozen Puddle

Foxglove
Hollow

Stepping
Stones

Hedge End

Secret Den

To Hazelnut
Grove

Map of
Bluebell Woods

Chapter One

It was the last day of school before the winter break and Natalie Hollyhock's class were tidying up. Natalie was underneath a desk, reaching for a hazelnut shell. "This must have been here since our cooking lesson last week," she said, stretching a little further.

Her friend Evie Morningdew peered under the desk. "See if you can flick it to Honey, Nat!"

Natalie batted the nutshell. It whizzed across the classroom floor to their mouse friend Honey Pennyroyal, who was picking up seeds near the door. "Good shot, Nat," she called. She tossed the shell to Florence Candytuft, a rabbit, who was standing beside the bin.

Florence caught the nutshell and added it to the rubbish. "Are there any more?" she called, raising her voice to make herself heard above the hubbub. Everyone was in high spirits at the thought of breaking up, and the classroom rang with laughter and loud voices.

"No, just that one," Evie called back. "Want a hand to get out, Nat?" She lifted one end of the desk so Natalie could crawl out without getting her prickles caught.

"Thanks!" Standing up, Natalie looked round the classroom. Reggie, Evie's little brother, and his friend Peter were aiming

paper darts at the far side of the classroom,
and she ducked as one flew over her head.

Harvey and Albie, Honey's twin
brothers, were flicking each other with
dusters.

"Those two, honestly!" groaned Honey,
as she and Florence came over.

"It's lucky Mr Hazelgrove's in a good
mood," said Evie. Their teacher was
humming cheerfully to himself as he
tidied his desk.

"He's probably glad he won't have to nag you about your homework for a while, Evie," said Honey.

"I do it *sometimes*," Evie said, laughing.

Monty Hornbeam, a shrew, walked past carrying a conker. "How's your amazing, weather-forecasting nose, Monty?" asked Evie. "Is there snow on the way?"

"Weather-forecasting nose?" Natalie echoed, puzzled.

"Yes, it tingles when it's about to snow," Evie explained. "Monty gets it right every winter. Of course, you don't know about it because you're always asleep by then. Worse luck!"

Natalie and her parents went into hibernation every year as soon as the weather turned cold, and they didn't wake up until spring. "I know," Natalie sighed.

"I miss out on all the winter fun."

"So what about this snow, Monty?" asked Evie. "Any sign?"

Monty rubbed his long nose. "Not yet," he said.

"It must snow soon," said Florence. "This is the coldest it's ever been at the end of term."

"I'm already feeling sleepy," Natalie said, stifling a yawn. "And this morning my dad was talking about going into hibernation in a few days."

"Oh no," said Florence, disappointed. "I had hoped you'd get to play in the snow with us this year, Nat."

"Perhaps it'll snow tomorrow," Honey said hopefully.

Just then, Mr Hazelgrove clapped his paws and everyone turned to look at him.

"Thank you, everybody. The classroom is tidy now," he said. "I would like to wish you a very happy winter holiday. Class dismissed. Don't forget to wrap up warmly, it's bitterly cold outside."

Cheering and whooping, everyone headed for the coat racks. Natalie pulled on her thick woollen coat and stepped out into the cold. It was a bright day, and the sky was blue and cloudless. *Monty's nose was right*, she thought. She was sure it would have to be cloudy for snow to fall.

Reggie and Peter came bundling out of the door. "Race you back to my house," cried Reggie. "Last one there's a nutmeg!" They dodged round Natalie, then charged away.

Bluebell Woods

"Hurray!" Evie cheered. "No more school till spring!" Linking arms, the four friends skipped along the path that led to Primrose Meadow.

"I hope it does snow soon," said Florence. "I can't wait to go sledging."

"And play snowballs," said Evie.

"And go skating!" Honey exclaimed.

"That all sounds wonderful," said Natalie wistfully.

"It is!" her friends chorused.

Bluebell Woods

If only I could do all those things with them, Natalie thought. *If only there was some way I could stay awake…*

"We really miss you when you hibernate, Nat," Florence said.

Natalie sighed. "And I always feel as if I've missed out when I wake up in the spring. Not that I mind you having fun," she added hastily. "I just wish I was having fun with you."

"Fingers crossed that the snow comes tomorrow, then," said Honey. "Then we can all play in it together."

Suddenly, Natalie had an idea. *What if I stay awake longer than usual this year?* she thought. *Just for a few days, so I can go sledging and skating and throw snowballs.* It was so cold there was bound to be snow soon.

Bluebell Woods

A shiver of excitement ran through her prickles. She couldn't think of anything she'd like more than playing in the snow with her friends. But she'd have to persuade her mum and dad to let her stay awake.

"You're very quiet, Nat," said Evie. "Are you OK?"

"Yes, I'm fine. It's just … I need to go home."

Her friends stared at her, surprised. "Only for a while," Natalie said hurriedly. She didn't want to tell them her idea and get their hopes up, in case nothing came of it.

"Shall we come, too?" asked Florence.

"No, I'll meet up with you later. Where will you be?"

"It's too cold to play out," said Honey,

blowing into her cupped paws to warm them. "Let's go to our den. It'll be warmer there, and we might not be able to visit it for a while once it starts snowing."

"I'll see you there in a bit," Natalie promised. *And hopefully I'll have some good news to share*, she thought, as she hurried away through the woods.

chapter Two

"If only it would snow tomorrow while Natalie's still awake," said Honey to Evie and Florence, as they made their way to the den.

"We shouldn't keep going on about snow," said Evie. "We don't want to get Nat's hopes up."

"Well, I still think—" Honey started.

"Where did that come from?" interrupted Florence, pointing to a wide, shallow puddle not far from the Stepping Stones that crossed the Babbling Brook.

"It's been pretty wet lately," Evie said.
"Think of all the rain we had last night.
And yesterday. And the day before. No
wonder there's a puddle."

"It's more like a lake than a puddle!"
said Florence, as the friends edged round it.

They leaped across the Stepping Stones,
then ran to their secret den. It was inside a
hollow ash tree, not far from the Babbling
Brook. Checking that nobody was about,
the friends squeezed through the opening
in the twigs that hid the den's entrance and
crawled up the narrow passage.

Florence lit the lantern. "Who fancies
a game of cards?" said Evie, plopping down
on a beanbag.

Florence nodded. "Good idea."

"But first let's see if there are any biscuits
left," Honey said, reaching for the tin.

Bluebell Woods

When Natalie reached her nest,
Blackberry Snug, she found her mum and
dad in the living room, sitting by a roaring
fire. "Come and get warm, darling," said
her mum. "Would you like a hot drink?"

"Yes, please," replied Natalie, taking
off her coat. She put a cushion in front of
the fire and sat down, holding out her
paws to the flames.

"Your mum and I have been talking about this cold weather," Dad said. "We've decided to go into hibernation earlier than usual this year. Tomorrow night, in fact."

"That soon?" Natalie said, horrified.

"It feels like the right time," said Mrs Hollyhock. "It's getting hard to stay awake. Dad's been dozing by the fire all afternoon." She went into the kitchen and returned with a steaming mug of elderflower cordial. "Here you are," she said, handing it to Natalie.

"Thanks, Mum." Natalie sipped her drink slowly, trying to work out the best way to tell her mum and dad her idea. It was such bad luck that they'd made up their minds to hibernate early. Now she'd have to work extra hard to persuade them to let her stay awake.

She set her mug on the hearth, then smiled awkwardly. "I was wondering…" She tailed off, not sure how to go on.

"What is it, darling?" Mum said gently.

"Well…" Natalie broke off again. She had to make them understand how badly she wanted to play with her friends in the snow.

Her parents looked at her, puzzled. "What's up?" asked Dad.

"Everyone's talking about snow," said Natalie.

Mr Hollyhock shivered. "No wonder. It's so cold I can hardly wait to snuggle down in my warm bed for the winter."

Natalie took a deep breath. "My friends plan to go skating and sledging," she said. "Do you think…? I mean … can we stay awake a bit longer so I can join them?"

She gazed hopefully at her parents. "Please. It sounds like brilliant fun."

Mr Hollyhock frowned. "Hedgehogs always hibernate when the weather turns cold, Natalie."

"I know, but—"

"And staying awake's difficult. Cold weather makes us sleepy."

"Just for a few days," Natalie begged. "Everyone says it will snow soon."

Mr Hollyhock yawned widely. "I can't see how we'll be able to stay awake, even if it is only for a few days."

Natalie sighed. She did feel tired, but she was sure she could stay awake with the snow to look forward to.

"My family delayed going into hibernation until Midwinter's Night when I was your age," said Mum thoughtfully. "We stayed up for a big party to celebrate finishing the new school."

"Old Oak School?" Natalie asked. "Was that built when you were young?"

"Yes. The tree came down in a storm and everyone worked away for weeks, hollowing it out. And it snowed the day before Midwinter." Mum smiled at the memory. "It wasn't easy to stay awake, but I had a wonderful time with my friends." She turned to Mr Hollyhock. "Why don't we stay up until Midwinter's Night, like I did all those years ago."

"Please, Dad," Natalie begged. "Midwinter's only three days away."

"We'll need extra food," Dad said.

"And what about firewood?"

"We've got stacks of food in the larder," said Natalie.

"And we can collect extra firewood," added Mum.

Mr Hollyhock sighed. "I suppose we can try staying awake. But only until Midwinter's Night. That's when we're going into hibernation – snow or no snow!"

Natalie jumped up and hugged her

parents. "Thanks, Mum. Thanks, Dad!" She ran to fetch her coat. "Can I go and tell my friends?"

"Of course," said Mum. "But make sure you're home before dark."

"I win!" cried Evie, scooping up a pawful of cards. "Oh, there you are, Nat!" She smiled as Natalie came into the den and shuffled up on the beanbag to make space for her.

"I've got something to tell you," said Natalie, beaming as she sat down beside Evie. "We're going to stay awake until Midwinter's Night, so hopefully I'll be able to play in the snow with you."

"Fantastic!" Honey cheered.

"How did you persuade your mum and dad?" asked Florence.

"Dad wasn't keen!" Natalie laughed. "But I managed to talk him round."

"Now, what are we going to do when it snows?" said Evie. "We've got to make sure you have the best time ever!"

"Sledging," said Florence. "There's nothing better than that."

"And there's the Midwinter snow-animal competition," said Honey.

"What's that?" Natalie asked eagerly.

"Everyone makes animal statues out of snow and on Midwinter's Day the judges give a prize for the best one," explained Honey.

"But only if it's snowed by Midwinter's Day, of course," Evie added. "If it hasn't, the competition takes place as soon as there's enough snow."

"That sounds brilliant," said Natalie.

"It'll be great having you around," said Florence, squeezing her paw.

"Let's have another biscuit to celebrate!" said Honey, reaching for the tin.

As they munched their biscuits, the friends told Natalie all about snow – how pretty it looked and how much fun it was.

Soon Natalie began to yawn loudly. "I just hope I can stay awake. Dad said it would be difficult."

"You'll be OK if you keep busy," Evie said. "And there'll be lots to keep you busy once it snows."

They went on making plans until Florence noticed that Natalie's head was drooping and her eyes had closed. "Nat," she said, shaking her arm gently.

Natalie lifted her head sleepily. "Is it time to go home?" she asked.

"Yes," said Florence. "The fresh air will wake you up."

"Perhaps we could collect some firewood while we go through the woods," Natalie suggested, as they put on their coats. "We need more wood."

"We've got a massive stack at home," said Florence. "I'm sure my mum and dad can spare some."

"And mine," said Honey and Evie together.

"Thanks," Natalie said.

The friends took a last look round the den, then blew out the lantern and crawled back down the passage and out into the chilly air.

"It's sad that we might not come back for months," sighed Honey. "We've had loads of fun here."

"Look out!" shouted a voice, as they neared the Babbling Brook.

Bluebell Woods

They leaped aside
as Reggie and Peter
came racing past.

"Reggie seems
happier now Peter's
moved into the village,"
Natalie said. "How are his family settling
in, Evie?"

Peter was Evie and Reggie's cousin, and
it was Evie who'd persuaded his parents to
move to the village. "Fine," she replied.
"The Brambles' old drey suits them
perfectly. And Reggie's back to his old
bouncy self now he's got a new friend to
play with."

They crossed back over the Stepping
Stones. "I'm going home to knit myself
some mittens," said Natalie, wide awake
now. "I've got a feeling I'll need them in

the next few days. See you all tomorrow." She hurried away.

"I hope she doesn't fall asleep too soon," Florence said anxiously.

"We'll just have to make sure she doesn't," said Evie. "Maybe we can go round in the morning to check that she's up."

"But she's already so sleepy, half the day will have gone by the time she's dressed and had breakfast," said Honey. "She needs someone to wake her up earlier."

"Mr Chervil!" Evie exclaimed. Mr Chervil was the Bluebell Woods postman and he lived next door to Florence. "Can you ask him to knock on Natalie's door when he's delivering their post, Florence? That should wake her up."

"I'll do it now," said Florence. "See you in the morning."

Bluebell Woods

As soon as she got home, Natalie fetched her knitting bag from her bedroom. "What are you making?" asked her mum, as she tipped the contents of the bag out on to the kitchen table and sorted through the brightly-coloured balls of wool.

"Mittens. I want to be warm while I'm playing in the snow."

"That will take a while," said Mum. "Can I help?"

"Yes, please." Natalie fished out two balls of green wool and gave one to her mum. "Let's make one mitten each."

Mum fetched a pattern. "These mittens are quite plain," she said, "but it'll be quicker if we don't try anything fancy."

"Just as long as they keep my paws warm!"

"Shall I knit you a matching scarf?" asked Dad.

"Thanks, that would be great!" Natalie found another ball of green wool and handed it to him.

"Let's have dinner before we start," said Mum. "The chestnut stew is just about ready."

They ate quickly, then sat by the fire, their knitting needles clicking as they worked. Natalie felt deliciously warm and she soon found her eyes closing. She sat up straighter and tried to concentrate on her knitting to keep herself awake.

"I wonder if it's snowing," she said. She went to the window, pulled back the curtain and stared out into the darkness.

Bluebell Woods

"Not yet," she sighed.

"I'm sure it will snow soon," said her mum, stifling a yawn. "I hope so, anyway. You'd love sledging. I tried it that year I stayed awake and it was wonderful."

Suddenly, there was a loud snore. Dad had fallen asleep in his chair.

"I think you might have quite a wait for that scarf!" Mum laughed.

"Never mind," said Natalie. "At least my paws will be warm. And I can always turn my collar up if my neck gets cold."

Bluebell Woods

By bedtime, Natalie had knitted half a mitten. "I'll finish it off this evening – if I can stay awake!" said Mum. "This one's nearly done."

"Thank you! It looks good," Natalie said. She kissed her mum goodnight, then headed for her bedroom. After changing into her pyjamas, she gazed out of the window, hoping to see snowflakes falling. But the bramble thicket looked just the same as always, with not even a hint of whiteness.

Natalie made a silent wish as she climbed into bed. *Please, please, PLEASE, let it snow soon.*

Chapter Three

Natalie was woken the next morning by a knock on the front door. She yawned and stretched, then rolled over, intending to go back to sleep.

Suddenly, she remembered that it might have snowed. She sprang out of bed, flung open her curtains and looked outside. The ground was white! Hurriedly, she pulled on her clothes and ran into the kitchen.

Dad was sitting at the table reading a letter. "That was Mr Chervil at the door," he said sleepily.

Bluebell Woods

"It's snowed!" Natalie told him, throwing open the living-room curtains and peering out. The bramble canes arching above Blackberry Snug were covered in glittering white. "Oh!" she gasped. "It's so pretty."

Grabbing her coat, she dashed to the door, but Dad called her back. "You can't go out without breakfast," he said.

"Oh, but…"

"The snow will still be there when you've finished." Yawning, Dad opened the oat jar. "A big bowl of steaming wild oat porridge will set you up for a day in the cold," he said.

Mum came out of the bedroom just as Natalie was finishing her breakfast. "Here you are, darling," she said, handing Natalie her mittens.

Bluebell Woods

"You've finished them!"
Natalie cried delightedly.
"Thanks, Mum." She
tried them on. They
fitted perfectly.

"Your scarf's not ready, I'm afraid,"
said Dad. "I couldn't keep my eyes open
last night. But I'll get it done today."

"Thanks." Natalie pulled on her coat
and mittens. As she opened the front
door, she spotted her friends coming to
call for her. She dashed to meet them.
"Snow!" she cried. "I've seen snow, at
last!"

"Oh, Nat, this isn't snow…" said Evie
gently.

"Not snow?" Natalie stared at her.

"No." Evie slipped her arm round
Natalie. "It's frost. A really heavy one."

A wave of disappointment washed over the little hedgehog. "I was sure…" She looked down, embarrassed at making such a silly mistake.

"I thought it had snowed, too, when I looked out this morning," said Florence kindly. "Everything's white. The crab apple tree near my house is smothered in frost."

"My dad says it's a hoar frost," Honey said. "It's frozen dew."

"So we won't be able to go sledging today?" asked Natalie sadly. Listening to her mum talk about sledging had made her more determined than ever to try it.

"No," said Honey. "But it's so cold it must snow soon."

Bluebell Woods

"What do you think of my new mittens?" asked Natalie, as she and her friends made their way out of the bramble thicket.

"They're a lovely colour," said Honey.

"You'll need them today," Florence said, rubbing her paws together to warm them. "It's freezing!"

As they reached Primrose Meadow, the sun came out from behind a cloud. Natalie gazed round, open-mouthed. Every blade of grass, and every branch of every tree bordering the meadow, was coated thickly with twinkling frost. "It's magical!" she gasped.

The friends stood and stared, spellbound.

"I'm getting cold," Evie said at last. "Shall we play on the Stepping Stones?"

"Good idea," they all agreed.

They ran towards the Babbling Brook, then came to a dead stop. The huge puddle they'd found yesterday was frozen solid.

"We could skate on this!" cheered Honey.

"Oh yes!" Florence cried. "You'll love skating, Nat."

Evie tested the ice with her foot. "It feels firm," she said. "And even if it gives way, the puddle's not deep. We'd only get wet feet if the ice did crack."

"I haven't got any skates," Natalie reminded them.

"You can wear Hattie's old pair," Honey said. "Let's all go and get our skates and meet back here."

Honey took Natalie's paw and they raced round to her nest, Hedge End.

Throwing open a cupboard in the hall, Honey pulled out a jumble of old toys. "The skates are here somewhere…" she said, rummaging impatiently.

At last, she found two pairs of skates and they dashed back to the frozen puddle. Florence and Evie were already there, sitting on a twig and fastening their skates.

"I hope mine fit," Honey said. "They were a bit big last year." She slipped them on and stood up, wobbling. "They're fine," she said, relieved.

Evie helped Natalie lace up Hattie's skates. "They could have been made for you, Nat!" she exclaimed.

Natalie took a step, but couldn't get her balance and fell over. "How on earth do you move on these thin blades?" she asked.

Bluebell Woods

"You'll soon get the hang of it,"
Florence said. She and Evie took hold of
Natalie's arms and pulled her up.

"Whoa! Don't let go!" she quavered, as
they helped her step on to the slippery ice.
They skated into the middle, towing
Natalie between them.

"Don't look so scared, Nat," Honey
said. "It's easy." She glided round them
with one leg in the air. "See."

"That doesn't look too hard," said Natalie. "Shall I try by myself now?"

"Why not?" said Florence. "Hold your arms out to balance." She and Evie let go of Natalie and gave her a gentle push. She slid forward, her arms sticking out stiffly, then plopped down on her bottom.

"It's not as easy as all that!" She giggled as her friends pulled her up. "But I'm determined to learn how to do it." She slid one foot forward and fell over again.

"Keep trying, Nat," said Honey, as they all helped her to her feet.

With lots of encouragement and advice from her friends, it wasn't long before Natalie could skate a few steps. "Look at me!" she cried happily, wobbling forward.

Bluebell Woods

"Brilliant, Nat!" Evie cheered.

More young animals began to arrive, and soon the ice was crowded with skaters. "I wish I could skate all the way round without falling over," Natalie said wistfully, watching them zoom by.

"Practice makes perfect," said Honey, doing a spin.

Florence linked arms with Natalie. "We'll go round together," she said.

Evie and Honey joined on, too, and the four of them skated right round the edge of the puddle.

"This is amazing!" Natalie cried, as they shot past Reggie and Peter.

But as they completed their third circuit, Natalie began to yawn.

"I'm starting to feel sleepy," she said, yawning again. "I'll sit down for a bit."

"You've got to stay awake," said Evie. "You don't want to hibernate before the snow comes."

"Let's have some races," Florence suggested. "That'll wake you up."

"I'll see who wants to join in," said Evie. She sped away across the ice, her skates glinting in the sunlight.

She came back with Reggie and Peter, Sophie Chervil, Florence's cousin Billy, Hattie, Tamsin Clover and Luke and Lily Willowherb.

"The race is two laps of the puddle," announced Honey. "Here's the finishing line." She threw down her hat on the frosty ground beside the ice. "The first one to pass my hat twice is the winner."

"Come on, Nat," Florence said, as everyone lined up.

"I won't win!" Natalie laughed, her
tiredness forgotten.

"Ready, steady, go!" cried Honey.

The other animals sped off, leaving
Natalie, Florence, Honey and Evie far
behind. "Don't wait for me," Natalie said.
"You might win if you skate fast."

"We'd rather skate with you," said
Florence firmly. Linking arms, they set off

after the others, but were only halfway round when those in the lead overtook them. By the time they reached the finishing line, Sophie was already organizing the next race.

"It's a relay," she called. "Teams of four."

"That sounds like fun," said Honey, as they lined up.

"Ready, steady, go!" Sophie shouted.

Evie skated first and finished ahead of the other competitors. She touched paws with Florence, who sped away at top speed.

"Now you, Nat," Florence cried, stretching to touch Natalie's paw.

Natalie wobbled away and fell over. By the time she'd got to her feet again, all the other racers had overtaken her.

"Go on, Nat! You can do it!" shouted Honey. Natalie made her way round the ice cautiously, falling over once more before she reached Honey.

Hattie and Tamsin's team had already finished the race, but Honey set off quickly, hoping to beat Reggie, who was halfway round. She caught up with him at the finishing line.

"Wow! You were fast, Honey!" cried Florence.

"And you look wide awake again, Nat," said Evie. "And that was what we wanted."

"No wonder I'm wide awake!" Natalie giggled. "It's freezing. The wind's blowing right down my neck." She turned up her collar.

"You need a scarf," said Florence.

"My dad's trying to knit me one," Natalie said. "But he keeps falling asleep."

"Let's go and see if he's finished it yet," suggested Honey. "Then we can get warm by your fire."

Bluebell Woods

They took off their skates and ran round to Blackberry Snug, where Mr Hollyhock was fast asleep in an armchair by the fire. The scarf, which was resting on his lap, was not even half finished.

"Poor Dad," Natalie said. "He's finding it a real struggle to stay awake."

They sat down by the fire, stretching out their frozen feet to warm them. Natalie made mugs of hot blackcurrant cordial and handed round walnut cookies. Then she picked up her dad's knitting.

 "I'll do a bit more of this while we're warming up. If I wait for Dad to finish it, it won't be ready till summer!"

Soon, they were as warm as roasted chestnuts. "That's better," Honey said with a contented sigh.

"Shall we go out again?" Evie asked, standing up. "We could find Monty and ask about his weather-forecasting nose."

"Yes, let's!" Natalie finished her row, then put the knitting back on her dad's lap.

As they were leaving the room, she saw that he was stirring. He yawned and stretched, then looked down at the scarf. "Well I'm blessed!" he exclaimed. "I didn't realize this scarf was so long. I must have been knitting in my sleep."

Natalie smiled to herself and crept out.

They soon found Monty; he was standing in the middle of Primrose Meadow, rubbing his nose.

"Hello, Monty," the friends chorused.

"Hi," he said.

"Is your nose tingling?" asked Honey.

"Like billy-o," he replied, nodding. "Snow must be on its way."

Excitedly, Natalie looked up at the sky. Dark clouds were building up along its northern edge. "Yippee!" she cried, hugging herself to keep warm. "It's going to snow! At last!"

Chapter Four

Next morning, when Natalie opened her bedroom curtains, there was a pile of fluffy bluey-whiteness heaped up on the outside window sill. "Snow!" she gasped, standing on tip toes to peer outside.

Now she could see the bramble thicket, but it was transformed into a strange landscape of smooth white curves and hollows. The blackberry canes were snowy pillars and the ground between them looked as soft and inviting as an eiderdown.

Bluebell Woods

Natalie quickly got dressed and raced into the kitchen. "It's snowed!" she cried, pulling on her coat.

Her mum was making porridge. "Breakfast's nearly ready," she said, smiling at Natalie's excitement.

"I can't stop for breakfast," Natalie cried. "I want to get round to Honey's. We can go sledging and start on our snow animals."

"Take one of these then," Mum said, handing her a hazelnut bar. "It should keep you going until lunchtime."

Bluebell Woods

Natalie put it in her pocket. Her new scarf was neatly folded on the kitchen table. "My scarf's finished!" she exclaimed, wrapping it round her neck and tying it securely. "Where's Dad?"

"Clearing a way out," said Mum. "We've been snowed in."

Natalie pulled on her mittens and opened the front door. A path sloped up away from the door, with high snow-walls on either side. Dad was digging hard, tossing snow to one side with his spade. "Nearly there," he called. "I never realized snow could be so much work!"

Natalie scampered up the slope. "Thanks for the scarf, Dad. It's lovely and warm." She kissed his cheek.

"Glad you like it! What do you think of the snow then?" he asked, starting to dig again.

"It's beautiful!" Natalie sighed happily. The sky was bright blue and the sun was shining down between the blackberry canes, setting the snow glittering. She sniffed deeply. "And it smells so fresh and clean and new."

She took off one mitten and touched the snow. It was cold, but very soft. She tossed a pawful up in the air and watched it drift down again in a powdery shower. Catching a flake on her tongue, she let it melt into her mouth. "It tastes fresh, too. And look!" she exclaimed, spotting the trail of footprints she'd left behind her. "I can make pretty footprint patterns." She took tiny steps so her footprints were

close together, then huge
ones. When she jumped, her
feet sank into the snow,
leaving deep holes.

Her mum looked out of the front door.
"Aren't you going to call for Honey?"

"Yes," Natalie replied. "It's just…" She
bumped against a blackberry cane and a
dollop of snow plopped down on her head,
making her giggle. "I didn't realize how
amazing snow would be!"

"Wait till you go sledging," said her
mum. "That was my favourite thing of all."

"Sledging, yes! I'm off to Honey's now!"

Natalie raced round to Hedge End,
leaving a footprint trail right across
Primrose Meadow.

Honey was already outside. "Isn't it
fantastic!" cried Natalie, dashing up to her.

"Everything looks so lovely and I've been making footprints and…" She broke off breathlessly as she noticed Honey was brushing dust and cobwebs off a wooden object. "Is this your sledge?" she gasped.

"That's right," said Honey, beaming at her friend's excitement. "Give me a hand cleaning it, then we can go sledging."

Grabbing a cloth, Natalie wiped furiously at some sticky cobwebs underneath the sledge.

"That should do it," said Honey, giving the runners a final polish. "We'll go faster with clean runners." She set the sledge down on the snow. "You go first, Nat. I'll pull you."

"Thanks!" Natalie sat on the sledge and Honey took hold of the honeysuckle-stem rope. She tugged hard and the sledge lurched forward. "Whoa!" Natalie cried, gripping the sides tightly.

"You think this is fast – just wait till you go downhill!" Honey laughed. She jogged towards Florence's house and the sledge glided smoothly after her.

Natalie gazed round at Primrose Meadow as she rode along. It looked completely different in the snow, with everything smothered in white. Up ahead, she could see that snow had drifted against the front wall of Meadowside Burrows. It was so deep that the windows were blanketed almost to the top, and a pathway had been cleared to each front door.

Bluebell Woods

"Hello," said Florence, flinging open the door to her burrow and placing her sledge on the ground. "Let's go to Foxglove Hollow – it's the best place for sledging. We can knock for Evie on the way."

Foxglove Hollow was already crowded with young animals when the four friends got there. They were swooping down the steep sides on their sledges, whooping excitedly. Luke Willowherb and Monty were racing each other, leaning forward as they tried to edge in front. Reggie and Peter were trudging up the slope, pulling their shared sledge behind them.

Natalie stood up. "Thanks for pulling me here, Honey. It was a great ride!"

"Stay on," Honey said. "Then you can go downhill."

"No, you go first," said Natalie. She was itching to sledge down the slope, but it was only fair to let Honey go first after she'd let Natalie ride all the way here.

"Are you sure?" asked Honey. "I don't mind waiting."

"Neither do I," Natalie said firmly.

They found a space at the top of the slope and checked that it was clear below. Honey jumped on her sledge. "Here I go!" she squeaked. She pushed off and sped away down the hill.

"I'm next," said Evie, whizzing after her.

"You can share my sledge, Nat," said Florence. "It's a bit bigger than Honey's and Evie's."

"Are you sure there's room for both of us?" Natalie asked doubtfully. It didn't look particularly big.

"Of course," said Florence. "But I'll sit in front. Otherwise I'll be squashed up against your prickles." She sat on her sledge and Natalie squeezed on behind her.

"We're next!" cried Florence. "Push off with your feet, Nat." Natalie did as she was told and they zoomed down the slope, gathering speed as they went. "Yippee!" Florence cried.

Suddenly, Natalie felt herself slipping off the back of the sledge. She made a grab for Florence's coat, but she wasn't quick enough and the next moment she'd plopped down in the snow. Giggling, she stood up and brushed off her clothes. She saw that Florence was still whizzing down the slope, while Evie and Honey were waiting for her at the bottom.

The three of them dashed back up the slope to Natalie. "Sorry about that," said Florence. "Are you OK?"

"Fine. Can I have another go?"

"We'll have to squash up even more this time," Florence said, as they hurried back to the top. She sat on the sledge and Natalie climbed on behind her again. Determined not to fall off a second time, she wrapped her arms tightly round Florence's waist.

Bluebell Woods

"Here we go," Florence said, pushing off. They raced away, with Evie and Honey on either side. But halfway down the slope there was a loud crack. The sledge tilted, throwing Natalie and Florence into the snow.

"What was that noise?" asked Natalie, as Florence helped her to her feet. They turned the sledge over. One of the runners had snapped off.

"What bad luck!" groaned Florence.

Evie and Honey came scampering up the hill. "What's happened?" asked Evie.

"The sledge is broken," said Natalie. She was bitterly disappointed that she hadn't managed to sledge all the way down

the slope, but she felt bad for Florence,
too. If she hadn't been sharing the sledge,
the runner wouldn't have snapped. It just
wasn't strong enough to take two. She
squeezed Florence's paw. "Sorry."

"It wasn't your fault," said Florence.

Honey knelt down to examine the
broken runner. "There's no way we'll fix
this," she said glumly. "We'll have to take
it to Mr Hornbeam's."

Chapter Five

Mr Hornbeam, Monty's dad, was a carpenter. His furniture could be found in every home in Bluebell Woods, but in the winter he made and repaired sledges, too.

The friends hurried to his workshop, Underwood Cavern, a large underground chamber that smelled of sawdust and beeswax polish. Tables, chairs, cupboards and beds were all neatly arranged inside to tempt buyers. The friends found Mr Hornbeam right at the back, painting gold swirls on a beautiful red sledge.

"Wow!" exclaimed Honey. "Imagine having a sledge like that!"

Mr Hornbeam looked up. "Hang on, girls. I just need to finish this bit."

Natalie sat down on a chair while they waited. The workshop was warm after the cold outside and she felt a bit sleepy.

Mr Hornbeam put down his paintbrush. "What can I do for you?" he asked, smiling.

Florence and Evie showed him the broken sledge. "The runner's come off, Mr Hornbeam," said Florence. "Can you fix it, please?"

Mr Hornbeam examined the sledge. "The runner can't be mended. I'll have to replace it," he said. "But I'm afraid I can't do it today. I'm busy with this new sledge and I promised to have it ready by tomorrow."

"Oh dear," sighed Florence. She wanted Natalie to have a proper go at sledging before she went into hibernation. "Perhaps I should buy a new one instead."

"Sorry," said Mr Hornbeam. "I've been so busy making furniture for Wilbur and Alice Morningdew's new home that I haven't had time to make any yet."

"We'll just have to take turns on ours," Evie said.

"I suppose so," Florence said sadly.

"You don't mind sharing, do you, Nat?" asked Honey.

Natalie didn't reply.

They all turned to look at her and found that she'd fallen asleep. Evie shook her awake gently. "Hey, Nat."

Natalie yawned and rubbed her eyes. "Is Florence's sledge fixed now?" she asked hopefully.

"No, we'll have to take turns on the other two sledges," said Florence.

Leaving the broken sledge with Mr Hornbeam, they went back out into the cold.

"Let's have a snowball fight," suggested Honey. Florence was good at snowballing and she hoped a game would cheer her up. She scooped up a pawful of snow, moulded it into a snowball and threw it at Evie, hitting the tip of her tail.

Laughing, Evie threw one back.

"Missed!" Honey cried, skipping out of the way.

"What's the secret to a good snowball?" asked Natalie, eager to join in.

Florence showed her. "Press the snow together hard," she explained. "Otherwise the snowball falls apart when you throw it."

Natalie picked up some snow and neatly shaped it into a snowball. As she prepared to throw it, one of Honey's snowballs hit her on the arm. Quickly, she hurled her snowball, which hit Honey's front, leaving a snowy mark on her coat. "Got you back, Honey!" she said, giggling.

Bluebell Woods

They threw snowball after snowball,
ducking and dodging to avoid being hit,
and moving out from under the trees into
Primrose Meadow.

"This is really good fun," panted
Natalie, as she scooped up another pawful
of snow. "I'll have to stay awake every
winter from now on."

Florence made an extra big snowball
and threw it at Evie. Evie ducked and the
snowball skimmed over her head.

Bluebell Woods

"Missed!" she yelled.

"No, she didn't!" said a stern voice behind Evie. The friends whirled round. Mrs Wintergreen, the teacher of the older class at school, was brushing snow off her coat.

"Sorry, Mrs Wintergreen," gasped Florence. "I didn't see you there."

"Be more careful in future." Mrs Wintergreen marched away.

"That was bad luck," Evie said, when she'd gone.

"Never mind," said Natalie. "She'll have forgotten all about it by spring when school starts again. And she's not our teacher, anyway."

"How about we do something else?" Honey suggested. "Sledging again, or shall we start making our snow animals for the competition?"

Natalie didn't know which she'd enjoy most. She badly wanted to sledge all the way down the side of Foxglove Hollow, but she loved making things, too.

"Why don't we make a start on our snow animals?" said Evie. "And go sledging later. Is that OK with everyone?"

"Fine," they chorused.

"I wonder what the prize is?" Honey said. "Last year it was a beautiful kite – bright green with ribbons and bows. Sophie won it."

"Perhaps one of us will win this year," said Florence eagerly. "Come on, let's get started."

Chapter Six

The competition was being held near the
hazel bush in Primrose Meadow. The
friends hurried over and found that lots of
their school mates had left Foxglove
Hollow and were now busily building
snow animals. "This looks like fun," said
Natalie excitedly, as they found a space
beside Monty. He'd already built the body
of his snow animal; now he was working
on the head.

"Your nose was right about the snow,
Monty," said Evie. "Well done!"

"Thanks. What sort of animals are you all going to make?"

"One of us could do a mole," Honey suggested. "We made that great snow statue of Mr Hazelgrove last year. Do you remember?"

Florence and Evie laughed.

"But we've done a mole," said Florence. "I want to make something different. What are you making, Monty?"

"A badger," he replied.

"I might do an owl," said Evie. "Their heads are pretty well round so I could make it out of a big snowball."

"But if it's too easy you won't win," Honey pointed out.

"Why don't we make statues of ourselves?" Natalie suggested.

"Oh yes!" agreed Florence. She began to scoop snow into a heap.

They'd barely started on their snow animals when Mrs Hollyhock appeared, carrying a basket of carrot pasties. "There you are," she said. "I was on my way to Foxglove Hollow, so you've saved me the walk."

"Thanks, Mum," Natalie said.

"Brilliant!" Evie cried, taking a pasty. "Thanks, Mrs Hollyhock."

"We're entering a snow animal competition," Natalie told her mum. "There's a prize for the best one."

"Good luck!" Mum said. "I'm busy, too, preparing a hibernation feast for tomorrow evening. Dad said he'd help, but he's fallen asleep again." She laughed, then added, "I hope you'll all be able to come."

"Yes, please," chorused the friends.

When Mrs Hollyhock had gone, the friends sat on a broad twig and tucked into the steaming pasties.

"That was lovely," Honey said, brushing crumbs from her coat when they'd finished. "I feel all toasty inside now."

"Make the most of it!" Evie laughed. "Have you noticed the sky?" While they'd been eating, dark clouds had built up, blocking out the sun.

Bluebell Woods

As she finished speaking, a snowflake curled down from the sky and settled on Honey's hat. Another landed on Natalie's outstretched paw. "Is it a snowflake?" she asked, entranced.

"Yes," replied Honey. "They're pretty, aren't they?"

"Yes. Sort of … lacy."

"And cold," Florence added, tying her scarf tighter.

They returned to their snow animals and worked steadily, building up the bodies and shaping the arms, while snowflakes fluttered and danced around them.

At last the snow stopped falling, but now the light was beginning to fade. "It'll be dark soon," Natalie sighed. There was so much to fit in before she went into hibernation and the days were very short at this time of year.

They stood back to look at each other's snow statues.

"They're coming on really well," Honey said. "Except my wood mouse and your rabbit haven't got heads yet, Florence," she added, giggling.

"And I haven't done my squirrel's ears or tail," Evie said. "How are you doing, Nat? Yours looks nearly finished."

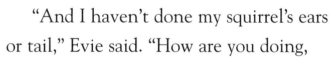

"All done except for the prickles. They're really tricky."

"We should come back first thing," said Florence. "Let's meet here straight after breakfast. The judging's at midday so we should have time to finish them before that."

"Right," they agreed.

Natalie couldn't stop yawning as she trudged home. Her dad was right about it being hard to stay awake. But she was glad she hadn't gone straight into hibernation – snow was wonderful! She couldn't wait to finish her snow hedgehog and hopefully there'd be time for some more sledging tomorrow, too. If only she didn't feel so sleepy…

Next morning, Florence, Evie and Honey
met up by the hazel bush to finish their
snow statues. "Hattie's heard that the prize
is a dress made by Mrs Buttercup," said
Honey excitedly. Mrs Buttercup was the
Bluebell Woods seamstress.

"Let's hope Monty doesn't win then!"
Evie giggled.

"How did Hattie hear about the prize,
Honey?" asked Florence.

"Her friend Tamsin overheard Mrs
Buttercup talking about a dress she was

going to make for a special occasion."

Florence laughed. "Honey, the Buttercup Stitchery is always making dresses for special occasions."

Honey's face fell. "I never thought of that. What a shame! I would have loved a new dress."

"I'm sure the prize will be something boys will want to win as well as girls!" Florence said. "Now, we'd better get going if we want to stand a chance of winning."

"I wonder where Nat is," Evie said.

"Her hedgehog's nearly finished," Honey pointed out. "Perhaps she decided to come a bit later. I suppose there's no point hanging around in the cold with nothing to do."

They carried on with their statues. Florence shaped a rabbit's head with two long ears, then lifted it on to the snow body. "Nearly done," she said.

"Me too," said Evie. She gazed across Primrose Meadow. "There's still no sign of Nat. Shall we go and fetch her? She won't want to miss the judging."

Leaving their statues, they raced round to Blackberry Snug. The curtains were closed and the front door was locked.

Honey banged on the door. "Nat, are you in there?" she shouted.

There was no answer.

"Let's knock and shout together," suggested Florence. She counted to three, then they hammered on the door and called Natalie's name at the top of their voices.

Bluebell Woods

Inside Blackberry Snug, Natalie woke up suddenly. Someone was calling and banging at the front door.

Still half asleep, Natalie crawled out of bed and shuffled to open the door. "I must have overslept," she said, as she saw her friends. "Thanks for waking me. I might have slept all winter if you hadn't come."

Her mum and dad emerged from their bedroom, yawning. "What's going on?" asked Mr Hollyhock sleepily. "This is the second time I've had to get up this morning. Mr Chervil knocked earlier, but I took the letters and went back to bed."

"I didn't even hear him," said Natalie.

"Come on, Nat," cried Evie. "The judges will be looking at our snow animals soon. We've got to go and finish them."

"Oh, I didn't realize how late it was!"

gasped Natalie. She ran back into her
bedroom and dressed as quickly as she
could, but she was so sleepy it was hard
to make her paws do what she wanted.

"Ready," she said, coming out at last.

"Your jumper's inside out and your
skirt's back to front, Nat!"
Honey giggled.

"Never mind. No one
will notice when you've got
your coat on," said Evie.

Natalie put on her coat, mittens and
scarf, grabbed a hazelnut bar for breakfast
and raced out after her friends.

When they reached the hazel bush,
Natalie set to work on her snow hedgehog
straightaway. Once her friends had finished
their animals, they came to see how she was
getting on.

"This is hopeless," she said. "These prickles are taking ages."

"Can't you turn it into a fox or something?" suggested Evie.

Natalie sighed. "It doesn't look much like a fox. But it doesn't look much like a hedgehog, either, with hardly any prickles."

Suddenly, Reggie came running up. "The judges are coming!" he cried.

Mr Hazelgrove and Mrs Wintergreen were walking towards the snow statues.

"Oh no!" Florence groaned. "Mrs Wintergreen's one of the judges."

"What's wrong with that?" asked Reggie.

"I accidentally hit her with a snowball yesterday," sighed Florence. "I won't stand a chance of winning."

"Neither will I," gasped Natalie. "I'm nowhere near finished."

"I wish we could help you," Evie said. "But it's probably cheating if you don't make the whole thing yourself."

"At least the judges are starting at the far end," said Florence.

Suddenly, Natalie's gaze fell on the hazel bush. "Hey, I could use twigs for the prickles."

They ran to the tree and snapped off tiny twigs, then Natalie quickly pushed them into the snow hedgehog's back and head. "That looks great," said Honey. "You just need some round the back of the neck."

"There's no time," said Florence. "Mr Hazelgrove and Mrs Wintergreen will be here any moment."

They were only two statues away.

"I've had an idea," Natalie said, taking off her scarf.

"What are you doing?" Evie said. "It's freezing!"

Natalie tied the scarf round the snow hedgehog's neck.

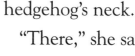

"There," she said, standing back to look at it. "The back of the neck's hidden now."

Mr Hazelgrove and Mrs Wintergreen walked over. "Hello, girls," they said.

The friends moved aside and watched anxiously as the two judges walked round their statues, inspecting them from every angle.

"I hope one of us wins," whispered Honey.

"Me too," they all agreed.

"That's all of them," Mrs Wintergreen

said. She spoke to Mr Hazelgrove in a low voice and he nodded.

"Gather round, everyone," he called loudly.

All the young animals came scurrying up and gazed hopefully at the judges.

"The winner of this year's competition is the snow hedgehog," Mr Hazelgrove announced.

"That's you, Nat!" squeaked Honey, dancing round her friend in delight.

"We loved the scarf, dear," said Mrs Wintergreen. "And the twig prickles. Very realistic!"

Mr Hornbeam appeared from behind a snowdrift. He was pulling the beautiful red and gold sledge that the friends had seen in his workshop.

"Here's your prize," Mr Hazelgrove said.

"The sledge?" Natalie gasped.

"That's right," said Mr Hornbeam, beaming broadly.

Natalie gazed at the sledge, hardly able to believe that it was really hers. She'd hoped to go sledging again, but she'd never expected to be able to ride on anything so beautiful. "Thank you!" she exclaimed. "It's perfect! And it's big enough for me and Florence to share."

Chapter Eight

"Yay!" cried Natalie as she and Florence
sped down the side of Foxglove Hollow
on the prize sledge. They zoomed past a
snowy bush at the bottom of the slope,
before gliding to a stop.

"Was it worth waiting for?" asked
Florence, as they scurried uphill again,
pulling the sledge between them.

"Definitely!" Natalie said. Everything
she and her friends had done together
over the last few days had been brilliant,
but sledging was the best of all – especially

when you were sharing your very own
beautiful red and gold sledge with one of
your best friends.

All too soon, the sky began to darken
and the other sledgers headed for home.
Natalie yawned. "Time for me to go, too.
I don't want to fall asleep at Mum's
hibernation feast."

"Let's have one last ride," suggested
Evie.

Foxglove Hollow was almost empty as
the friends positioned their sledges at the
top of the slope.

Natalie sat on the sledge behind
Florence and they pushed off and glided
down the hill, the wind ruffling their fur.
Honey and Evie set off at the same time,
but were soon left behind as the prize
sledge gathered speed.

Bluebell Woods

"That's the end of my winter then," said Natalie sadly, as they reached the bottom.

"Will you stay awake for a while next winter, too?" asked Evie, as her sledge slewed to a halt beside them.

"You bet!" Natalie yawned widely. "Come on, we'd better go."

Towing their sledges, they hurried across Primrose Meadow. "You can use my sledge while I'm hibernating, if you like, Florence," Natalie said.

Bluebell Woods

"Wow, thanks, Nat!"

As they reached Blackberry Snug, Natalie's mum opened the door. "Come in, everyone," she said. "Welcome to our hibernation feast."

They piled into the cosy living room. The table was set with round snowball cakes dusted with icing sugar, plates of sandwiches and, right in the centre, a cake with snowflake-patterned icing. "Yummy!" Honey said, her eyes widening with delight.

"We always have a big meal before we hibernate," said Natalie. "But this is the best one ever, because you're all here to share it."

By the time the food was all eaten, Natalie was yawning again. "Sorry," she said. "I can hardly keep my eyes open."

"You should get to bed, darling," Mrs Hollyhock said.

Natalie kissed her mum and dad, then she and her friends headed for her bedroom.

"Sleep well," her parents called after her.

Natalie changed into her pyjamas and climbed into bed. "I've had a wonderful time," she said sleepily, snuggling down under her thick quilt.

Her friends covered her with an extra blanket and tucked it in tight. "Are you warm enough, Nat?" asked Florence.

There was no reply.

"Nat?" Florence peered a little closer. "She's asleep already," she whispered.

"See you in the spring, Nat," they all whispered, as they tiptoed out.

"I'm going to miss Nat soooo much," said Honey, as they crossed Primrose Meadow. "But I'm glad she managed to stay awake long enough to play in the snow."

"She's made it a really fun winter," said Evie.

"Definitely!" Florence agreed. "Our very best winter ever!"